STELLA

CURVY GIRLS CAN

SADIE KING

LET'S BE BESTIES!

A few times a month I send out an email with new releases, special deals and sneak peeks of what I'm working on. If you want to get on the list I'd love to meet you!

You'll even get a free short and steamy romance when you join.

Sign up here:
www.authorsadieking.com/free

STELLA

CURVY GIRLS CAN BOOK FOUR

Jared

I'm looking for an investment, not a relationship. But when Stella Parker walks into the boardroom, I know I'm a goner. She's smart, funny, and gorgeous.

But can I convince her that mixing business and pleasure isn't always bad?

Stella

Fashion for the curvy girl: It's what I do, and it's what I've built my business around. Now I'm looking for the right investment to take it to the next level.

Jared isn't a typical businessman with his tight black t-shirt and arm tattoos. One look and I'm in danger of throwing away everything I've worked so hard for.

Can I keep my business and keep my heart closed, or will the rock star investor be too much to resist?

Stella is part of the *Curvy Girls Can* series. Short, sweet and steamy instalove stories about women with big curves, big attitudes, and big dreams and the OTT protective men who are man enough to love them.

Cover designed by Designrans.

www.authorsadieking.com

1

STELLA

I take a deep breath, but it does nothing to help the queasiness in my stomach.

"Miss Parker."

At the sound of my name being called, my heart rate jumps up a notch.

The receptionist looks at me expectantly, pristine in her well-fitted size 4 body-hugging pencil dress and shiny heels. Her makeup is perfect, and there's not a hair out of place.

I tuck a strand of my wayward hair behind my ear.

"That's me." My voice comes out as a squeak, and I cough quickly to clear my throat.

I pick up my laptop and sample bag, and it almost slides out of my sweaty palms.

I take a few deep breaths. "You got this, girl," I mutter.

I feel some sense of calm returning, and I force

myself to straighten my back and hold my head up. I can almost hear my mother's voice in my head telling me to stand up straight.

By the time I walk through the glass doors to the boardroom, I've got a confident stride and a smile on my face. You'd never know the turmoil that's going on inside me.

But it's a pretty big deal to go up against a board of investors who hold my entire future in their hands.

I've been in San Francisco for three days and had too many meetings to count, and not one person has liked my idea enough to invest. This is the last meeting of the trip, and if I don't get the funding I need I'll fly back home tomorrow and pack in my business. So yeah, I'm nervous as hell.

I set my laptop up on the boardroom table and plug it into their big screen.

"I'm Stella Parker, and I'm going to be presenting my business Dressing her Curves.

My gaze travels down the line of five men sitting opposite me. I'm disappointed there aren't any women, but I'm not surprised. There hasn't been a single woman in any of the meetings I've been to. I sigh inwardly. I hope these men understand fashion.

They look much the same as the other investors I've presented to--corporate suits, clean shaven, with close cropped hair. You could make a mold out of them.

Until I get to the man on the end. He's tall with broad shoulders, and he's wearing a black t-shirt which shows off the colorful ink of a full sleeve tattoo. His face is dark with stubble like he forgot to shave for a few days.

How did a guy that looks like he should be in a rock band end up as an angel investor? He looks about as out of place in this impeccably ordered boardroom as I do.

He's leaning back in his chair and eyeing me with a casual look that makes my stomach feel queasy again.

I must be staring, because one of the other men coughs, which I take as a hint to get on with it.

I click onto my first slide and begin.

"Fashion, style, what you wear; it's important to the 21st century woman, as can be seen by the popularity of New York Fashion Week." I show photos of the New York runways and the stick thin models with their clothes hanging off them.

"And yet 68% percent of American women are a size 14 or upwards."

I can see them switching off, and I sigh inwardly. I've never seen such an industry that's crying out for diversification. If there was a woman in the room, she would get where I'm coming from. But the men in their plain suits don't get it.

Except for the rock star on the end. He's staring at me intently, a slight frown on his face as if he's trying to figure something out.

"There are fashion lines already that cater to the so-called "plus sized" woman. They're at the back of the department stores, shoved in the corner. Or they're larger sizes of dresses designed for slimmer women that aren't flattering to the fuller figure.

"A survey of plus sized women found that they don't like going to the shops. They find it hard to find clothes that fit, and the experience isn't pleasant."

I click to the next slide, showing a screen shot of my website.

"What Dressing her Curves offers is not only clothing designed specifically for the plus sized figure, but a complete virtual shopping experience.

The rock star leans forward. He's gazing at me so intently that I feel a blush creeping up my neck.

"We offer virtual fashion consultations. The client is in the comfort of her own home. She shows the consultant her wardrobe and tries on her favorite outfits. The consultant suggests items from the online catalogue that will suit her particular figure and style."

"What's your return rate?"

I blink at the rock star. His voice is smooth as honey, and it throws me off momentarily. "About twenty percent." I'm finding it hard to look at him. He's making my palms feel sweaty again. "Which is good for online fashion," I add quickly.

"So they're happy with the suggestions from the consultant?"

"Yes, most of the time."

"How many consultants do you have?"

I swallow nervously. I'm not sure how much I

should tell them. I design the clothes, do the consultations, find customers, do the accounts, and build the website. All of it on my own.

"We're pretty lean. At the moment, I do the all the consultations. But that's what I want to expand. Train other women up and grow the business."

"What are your overheads?"

"Low. With no storefront, we can keep costs low."

"Where do you keep your merchandise?"

Damn, he's curious, which is exciting. I haven't been asked this many questions in all of my previous meetings combined.

"At the moment, it's in storage at my home." I don't add that my tiny one-bedroom apartment is crammed to the rafters with boxes of stock.

"What is your P&L for the last year?" one of the other men asks while stifling a yawn. It's a standard question, and I pull up the slide with the figures and take them through the numbers.

The only one paying attention anymore is the rock star looking guy. He jots down something on his notepad and asks a few more questions.

The last slide is a selection of the products and he leans in again, studying them intently. I've included a variety of items: a red evening dress, a casual blouse, and our most popular wide hip jeans.

I've brought real samples of each with me and I pull them out of the bag, holding them up one by one as I talk about the designs.

But they don't seem interested. Even the rock star is busy scribbling on his pad.

I wrap up quickly and ask for any questions.

"I think you've answered them all already," one of the men says. My heart sinks. That's the standard line which means 'we're not interested.'

I unplug my laptop and stuff the samples in my bag. "Thank you for your time," I say, trying to sound cheerful.

"Thank you, Miss Parker," says the rock star, barely looking up from whatever it is he's scribbling on his notepad.

With my laptop under my arm, I head out the door. Another failed investment meeting.

2
JARED

I watch her leave the boardroom, her long blonde hair swaying as seductively as her ass.

"Like the world really needs another fashion website," says Brad, one of the other investors. "Especially for big girls."

They all laugh, and I shoot Brad a dirty look.

He pushes his chair back. "Where are we going for lunch? I hear the sirloin at Charmers is good."

They start discussing the local lunch options, but it's like a dull buzz in my head. All I can think about is Miss Stella Parker. Her luscious body had me hard the moment she walked in the door. I had to pull my chair under the table so no one would notice.

But it's not just her body. I look down at my notes. I was running the numbers, and they look good. Her business idea is sound. It's different than what I usually invest in. It will be a high risk.

Six months ago I wouldn't have hesitated, but I've had a few investments go bad lately, and I can't afford to lose any more money.

But the numbers are too good. And her ass...

I push my chair back so quickly it nearly falls to the floor. I scoop up my notebook and bag and head out the door.

"You coming for lunch?" Brad calls after me, but I ignore him and the surprised laughs that follow me out the door. If they can't recognize a good business opportunity and a beautiful woman when she's right in front of their eyes, then all the better for me.

I hit the elevator button, but it's on the top floor. Impatiently I push open the door to the stairwell and take them two at a time.

By the time I get to the ground floor, I'm sweaty and panting. I look around and catch a glimpse of Stella heading out the revolving doors.

I run after her and push my way through to the outside. She's walking down the steps of the building.

"Miss Parker," I call, but she doesn't hear me.

I race down the steps calling her name. She stops abruptly and spins around. Her hair fans out behind her, catching in the sunlight. I'm out of breath already, but the sight of her almost finishes me off. She's stunning with wayward blonde hair, intelligent eyes, and plump lips. Her colorful outfit that hugs her curves unapologetically is like a breath of fresh air in this stuffy corporate business park, where all the women look like they fell from the same tree.

"Miss Parker," I pant.

"Call me Stella," she says, looking surprised.

"Stella, I'm Jared."

"I know who you are."

Of course she does. She would have done her homework for today. I take a moment to catch my breath, and she looks at me expectantly. "I like your idea."

Her face breaks into a wide smile that lights up her whole face. "Thank you."

"It's original, and it's got potential."

"Thank you," she says again, and I realize she's nervous. A thrill runs through me at the thought that I make her nervous. Then I realize that she's probably just nervous because she wants me to invest.

"I'd like to find out more about it. Talk details with you."

"That's great. Yes, we can do that."

"Have dinner with me tonight."

Her smile falters for a moment, and an adorable blush creeps up her neck. "A business dinner?"

I'd really like to buy her dinner to get to know her, to listen to her talk, to get her back to my place and out of that dress, but I sense she's weighing something here. She's trying to figure out if I'm just trying to get laid, or if I'm actually interested in the business. She doesn't need to know that it's both. I give her my most charming smile. "Yes, of course. To talk business."

"That would be great then."

"Which hotel are you staying at? I'll pick you up."

"I'm staying with friends actually. Just tell me where to go, and I'll meet you there."

I name a little Italian place off the main street. "See you there at eight."

She turns to go, and I call after her. "Stella."

She turns around.

"Wear the red dress."

She looks confused.

"The red dress from your samples."

"Oh." She smiles. "Sure."

3
STELLA

I stride toward the entrance to the restaurant with a confidence I don't feel. I'm not sure if I'm nervous about talking business or if I'm nervous about meeting Jared.

"It's just business," I mutter to myself, continuing the pep talk in my head. "Keep it purely business."

I catch my reflection in the restaurant window. I'm wearing the red dress as instructed. It looks good on me, the low cut showing off my cleavage and the wide skirt giving me a 1950s pin-up look. The deep red sets off my blonde hair, and I've put on lipstick to match the color.

I pull open the door and step inside.

"I knew you'd look good in that dress."

Jared is already here, looking hot in what must be his signature black-t-shirt and slacks.

His eyes travel over me appreciatively, and I feel a

thrill run through my body. Damn, this is no time to go all to pieces over a man.

"I made this for my cousin's wedding."

"You must have outshone the bride."

I laugh nervously, and he leans in to kiss my cheek. I get a heady whiff of aftershave. It's subtle and manly and just about makes me swoon.

Get it together, girl, I instruct myself in my head.

"Table for two?" the maître d' asks.

Jared nods, and the maître d' sets off across the restaurant. Jared indicates for me to go first, and as I swish past him, I hear an intake of breath.

I smile to myself. Because yes, this dress has a low back, and I am baring some flesh. I feel his eyes on my back as we cross the restaurant. And yes, I did tie my hair in a high pony especially so my back is exposed.

I'm proud of my body, and I like to show it off. At my cousin's wedding Mom was trying to cover me with a shawl the whole night, but I knew from the admiring glances I was getting from men and the dirty looks from women that I was onto a winning design.

I made some adjustments to the pattern and added it to my portfolio, and it's been one of my biggest sellers.

I wouldn't normally wear a dress like this to a business meeting, but he did tell me to, and who am I to argue with the man who may be about to invest in my business and change my life?

We get to the table, and I slide into my seat. Jared

sits across from me, and man, I'm going to find this hard to keep to business. I may have only seen him in a black t-shirt, but he knows how to wear it: tight, showing off his broad shoulders and muscular arms. But it's those tats I'm drawn to, the color contrasting with the black t-shirt. I can't help wondering what it would feel like being wrapped up in those arms.

I pick the menu up, because I suddenly feel tongue-tied. But he snatches it off me and leans forward, so I'm forced to look him in the eyes. They've got a mischievous twinkle to them.

"So, Miss Stella Parker, what do you mean by wearing a dress like that out to a business dinner?"

My eyes go wide with indignation. "You told me to wear it."

"I didn't know it was backless."

"You should have paid more attention in the presentation then."

He laughs. "I was paying attention, believe me." He sits back just as the waiter comes to take our order.

I pick up the menu again, but my mind's in a whirl. He's flirting with me, and I frickin' love it. My heart is racing, my stomach is doing double flips, and my panties are on fire.

This is not how you're meant to go about getting an investment.

Pull yourself together I instruct my head, my heart, and my stomach. But my treacherous body seems to be having too much fun.

I hold the menu up and take a few deep breaths. When I feel calmer, I lower the menu.

Jared is watching me curiously.

"I'll take the fettuccine alfredo," I say, trying to sound casual and as if it's perfectly normal to hide behind a menu for a quick spot of mindfulness during diner.

The waiter puts his hand out to take the menu, and I reluctantly hand it over. Nothing to hide behind now.

"So tell me how you got into fashion design," Jared says.

Thankful for a safe topic, I tell him all about my love of fashion and my frustration at not finding fashionable clothes in my size. How I started making my own, and then for my friends, and before I knew it, I had an Etsy store and was taking orders.

"How about the consulting?" he asks, as we dive into our main course.

"I had a lot of customers asking me questions about if they'd suit a certain style. They would send me photos of themselves and ask for help choosing some pieces. It seemed like the next logical step."

He's nodding as I talk. "They make the best businesses when they grow out of a passion like that."

"I just wanted to help people. Give them a personal shopping experience and clothing they'll look and feel great in."

His face turns serious all of a sudden. "I think

you've got a great business model, but your profits aren't what they should be."

I pause with my fork to my mouth. "What do you mean?"

"I went over your figures from today. There are places you could work leaner and opportunities for growth."

I'm very protective of my business and it's hard to take criticism, but I remind myself that he's the expert. "What do you mean?"

"This would make a good franchise business."

"Go on."

"You sell a license to individuals who run the business themselves."

I shake my head. "It sounds complicated. I wouldn't know where to begin."

"That's why you need a business partner. Someone with the expertise to take your business to the next level."

I put my food down. "What are you proposing?"

"I want to invest."

My heart jumps into my throat. This is what I've been waiting for. "Great, that's great."

"I'll give you half a million dollars." My mouth drops open. "And I want sixty percent."

My mouth snaps shut. I'm not giving up that much of my business to anybody. "Thirty percent."

"Fifty percent or there's no deal."

The twinkle is gone from his eyes, and his expression is hard. He looks even hotter when he's negotiating. "And I'll be your business consultant," he adds.

I really need his expertise, but I have to retain the majority share in the business; I've worked too hard for this. My insides are churning, but I set my face to hard-ass.

"Forty-five percent."

He squints at me, but I keep my expression hard. The moment seems to last forever.

"Done."

I let out a breath I didn't know I'd been holding. He holds out a hand, and I shake it. It's big and warm and firm, and I'm so excited I could kiss it. Instead I shake it like a maniac, unable to hide the huge smile from spreading across my face.

"I guess we'd better celebrate." His eyes are twinkling again as he calls the waiter over.

I'm still smiling when he hands me a glass of champagne.

"To Dressing Her Curves."

Our glasses knock together, and our eyes meet. Behind the laughter in his eyes there's something else I recognize, the dark look of desire.

"Do you want to go back to my place to continue the celebration?" he asks casually.

My heart starts knocking again, and there's a gush of wetness to my panties.

His hand strokes mine on the wineglass, and it's like an electric shock coursing up my arm. I'd like nothing more than to go back to his place, let him undress me slowly and show him how curvy girls do it.

Then I think of my business, of the hours I've spent working in my room, the late nights, all the times I've turned down nights out so I could work, how close I am to finally having all that hard work pay off. I won't risk ruining it for a night of passion.

He means more than that the voice in my head whispers.

Don't be so stupid, I tell her. I may have that sick feeling that I could be falling a tiny bit in love with Jared. But there's no way the rock star investor is thinking of me as anything more than a one-night stand with his new business partner.

It would be disastrous.

Ignoring my rebellious body and with all the resolve I can muster, I shake my head.

"I don't think that's a good idea."

Disappointment flashes across his face, but he doesn't push it.

"You're probably right," he says, leaning back.

"We shouldn't mix business with pleasure," I say, hating the way the cliché sounds on my tongue.

We pay the bill and stand up. His hand rests on the small of my back as he guides me through the restaurant, making my knees go all quivery.

We get outside, and he hails me a taxi. I get in, and before he shuts the door, he leans in.

"It wouldn't have just been one night, Stella. I hope you know that."

His lips brush mine. And then he straightens up and shuts the door. The driver pulls away, and I'm left with my lips burning and my mind racing as the taxi drives me away from the hottest man I've ever met.

4
JARED

It's been just over a week since I met Stella, but the imprint of her in that red dress is fresh in my mind. It haunts me at night when I'm lying alone in bed. I imagine unzipping it slowly, easing her out of it, and easing my cock into her sweet pussy.

She flew back to her hometown the day after we had dinner, so I never got an opportunity to explain. I didn't just want her body. There's something about this girl that makes me want the whole package. Body, mind, soul, and everything in between.

I pour myself a coffee and turn on my laptop. Maybe it's for the best. We shouldn't mix business and pleasure. But damn, I'm drawn to her in a way I can't explain, in a way that tugs at me deep down in the pit of my stomach.

"Good morning!"

She's already on the call looking bright and fresh and smiling, which is more than I can say for myself.

"Morning," I mumble, running a hand through my hair. One thing I've learned about Stella is that she's a morning person, like an up at 5 a.m. kind of morning person.

"How's your day going?"

"I've only been up for five minutes, so pretty good so far." I take a sip of coffee. I'm a night owl, up late and sleep late. But she insists on having morning video calls so she can get on with her work for the day.

I watch her smiling face on the computer screen; not a bad reason to get up in the morning.

"Did you manage to run those reports for me?" I ask, getting down to business.

"Just finishing them off. You'll have them in a few hours."

"Great. I've potentially found you the first franchise owner."

Her eyes light up, and I'm delighted by how happy that makes her. "Really? Who?"

"A woman I know, Karen."

Her mouth twitches, and I wonder if she's jealous. Not that there's any reason to be. "She's looking to start her own business, and I might have convinced her to buy a franchise."

"That's great!" Her face falls. "I'll have to get a training plan together and some more merchandise. I'm running out of space in my garage."

"Relax. It won't happen overnight. You've got time."

"Okay, okay. I do need to start thinking about the training though." She scribbles something on her notepad while I sip my coffee.

"So how are the new designs coming along?"

She talks excitedly about the new office wear range she's designing. It's not a part of the business I really need to know about, but I love seeing her this passionate.

The truth is that we don't really need to talk every day. But I suggested a daily video conference because I want to see her face, hear her speak. Get to know her. And so far, I like what I've seen. She's smart, funny, and so goddamn sexy.

I wonder what she'd think if she knew I was jerking off thinking about her in that red dress every night.

"Do you have any of the mockups?"

"You wanna see?"

"Sure."

She gets up from her desk and ducks behind a pile of boxes at the back of the room. She told me the boxes are full of next season's stock, which has just gone live on her site. From what I can tell, her whole business runs out of her small one-bedroom apartment.

She comes back with a garment that's loosely stitched together.

"This is a dress I'm working on. It's a wraparound, and I'm adding a bow to the side to take the focus away from the stomach area."

"Let's see it on."

She shakes her head. "Oh no, it's not ready."

"Come on, let's see. I'll give you my opinion as someone who's worked in the corporate world."

"All right. Back in a minute."

She goes behind the boxes again, but this time she's not quite out of site. There's a mirror back there and it's at just the right angle that I see a glimpse of her undressing.

I take a sip of coffee and smile. I'm sure she doesn't know I can see, but that's not going to stop me from enjoying the show.

I see a flash of leg as she steps into the dress and her back with a black bra across her skin. I can only see a glimpse of her, but it's enough to get my dick hard and my blood thumping.

Then she's dressed and back in front of the screen.

"What do you think?" she asks innocently.

I'm glad this is a video conference, because if she was in the room with me she'd see my raging hard-on. Damn, this woman is driving me crazy.

"It's perfect," I say, trying to focus on the dress and not the buxom goddess in it. "But if you wore that in the office, you'd have every man drooling after you and half the women too."

"Too much cleavage?" She pulls at the top of the dress.

"Yeah, too much."

"Hmmm." She chews her bottom lip thoughtfully.

"Maybe I can use this design for the evening wear range and just change the fabric."

"I think that's probably a good idea." My voice comes out croaky.

"I gotta go. I need to get back to work."

"So do I." I don't tell her that I'll be going back to bed to fantasize about her as I pull on my aching cock.

"See you tomorrow."

She waves at me from the screen, and I try to focus on her face and not the way her tits jiggle up and down.

"See you tomorrow."

5
STELLA

The crack of thunder wakes me with a start. The rain's coming down heavily, and the tree next to my room is scraping against the window. I pull the covers over my head, but I already know I'm not going to be able to get back to sleep.

There's a flash of lightning that illuminates the whole room. My bed's surrounded by boxes, and my eye catches on the fabric samples strewn over the top. I need to make some decisions on which patterns I want to go with.

Now that I'm awake my mind's on work, and I pull myself out of bed. If I'm not going to be able to sleep I may as well work.

I make a mug of coffee and open my laptop. I pull a blanket around me and sit down at my desk.

I've got a to do list as long as my arm, but the first

thing I do is check my messaging app. It's been over two weeks now that I've been working with Jared, and my heart still races every time I see a message or an email from him.

Sure enough, there's a message from him.

I heard there's a big storm heading your way. You okay?

It's from 1 a.m. I check my watch. Just over an hour ago. I know he's a night owl, so he may still be up. I message him back, just in case.

Thunder and lightning here. It just woke me.

The reply comes back instantly, and I feel a flutter in my stomach.

Get back to bed. You've got a lot to do tomorrow :)

I smile to myself. Over the last few weeks, we've gone from a daily business only video call to messaging each other any time about anything. I don't know if it's possible to fall in love with someone via messaging, but I think I'm pretty damn close.

Wish you were here to tuck me in, I type. Then I delete it and go with something safer.

I'm at the laptop looking at spreadsheets.

Better to stick to safe and boring. I've got no idea what his feelings are, but he probably has some swanky girlfriend anyway. And what's the point when we live so far apart? It's nice to have a crush on the hot investor who's saving my business, but the reality is that it'd never work.

Do you ever take a break?

Yes. I took my mom's cat to the vet today.

Hardly a break. Is the cat okay?

She's fine. Sprained her leg jumping on the chair. She's not very cat-like.

Lol. Seriously, you need a day off. Don't make me come up there and drag you away from work for the day.

Where would you take me?

My heart races. I've never been so forward with him. There's no reply for a few minutes, and I stare anxiously at the screen.

First, I'd take you for a walk somewhere out in nature, because you must be tired of staring at those boxes in your room. Then I'd take you to a movie, because I know you like classic movies but you don't have time to see them. Then I'd find the best Italian restaurant in your town and take you there

I stare at the screen. He's just described my perfect date. Is he being serious or is it more flirting? I decide to go down the lighthearted route.

Vinnies is the best Italian place. When should I make the reservation? :)

Tomorrow night.

Lol, sounds good!

I'm not joking.

I stare at the screen. My heart is racing. It's felt so good getting to know him the last few weeks, but he can't really be serious. He's not going to fly from San Francisco to here just to take me out to dinner.

I'll make the reservation.

Good. I haven't told you what I'll do after dinner...

Whoa, what?! I stare at the words on the screen. My blood starts pumping, and I feel a tug in my lady region.

Two weeks of looking at his disheveled appearance every morning has gotten me hot and horny. Do men know how good they look with mussed morning hair and stubble and in their causal sweatpants and t-shirt? *Keep calm, girl,* I tell myself.

What will you do after dinner...?

I've got a nervous tingle as I press send. My body's on fire wondering what he's going to come back with.

I'll take you back to your place. You would be wearing the red dress, of course, and I'll slowly unzip it while kissing your neck...

Holy shit! This is what I've fantasized about every night since I met him.

Go on...

My body's on fire, and I slide the blanket off my shoulders. I can imagine him undressing me slowly, and even though I'm here on my own, my body responds as if he's right here doing these things to me.

I'll unhook your bra and kiss your breasts, taking your nipples in my mouth.

Holy hell! My nipples go hard as I read the words, and there's a gush of wetness between my legs. I should be thinking about cyber security, but instead I slide a hand into my pajama bottoms and rub it against my damp panties. Luckily I'm good at typing with one hand.

What will you do next?

I'll pull your dress down so I'm kneeling in front of you and you can feel my hot breath on your thighs.

I rub my panties, imagining him on his knees in front of me. I don't know if sexting it a thing, but it looks like we're doing it.

What next?

I'll pull your lacy panties off and run my tongue over your pussy.

I slide my hand inside my cotton panties, making a mental note that if this fantasy ever turns to reality to make sure I buy some lacy underwear.

Don't stop.

I'll slowly lick your pussy, tasting your sweet juice as I slide a finger into your cunt.

Oh my god. He typed the c word, and it's so frickin' erotic that I forget to type.

Then I'd take you over to the bed.

Whoa, why stopping?

So that you can unzip my jeans...

Oh shit, yeah.

I'll pull out your cock and put it in my mouth.

Damn, I'm not good at this. How would I get his cock in my mouth if he's just laid me down?

Sounds good.

Okay, I guess this is fantasy, and inconsistencies in positioning aren't important.

I'll lick your cock slowly while you lick my pussy.

My tongue laps at your swollen pussy while my hand runs over your breasts.

Damn, he's good at this. As I rub my wet pussy, I find it easier to imagine what I'm doing to him, and I'm not sure which is turning me on more.

I suck at your cock, running my tongue from the base to the tip.

My tongue slides over your slit while I slide my finger inside you. Can you slide a finger inside you now?

Yes, I'm fucking myself with my finger.

God that's dirty, I wish I was fucking you.

I wish I had your cock in my mouth as you fuck me.

That's impossible, but I'll go with it. Imagine my tongue licking your clit as my finger slides in and out.

I'm sucking your cock while you fuck me hard.

I'm going faster, tasting your juices.

I'm going to cum.

Me too.

Fuck.

Ahhhhdklkjkljklfjklsjg;kfds

I stare at the screen panting as my pussy convulses against my hand. What the fuck just happened?

You there?

Yup.

That was intense.

Yup.

I wish I was there to tuck you into bed.

So do I.

I have to go. Sweet dreams.

Goodnight.

I shut down the laptop and crawl back into bed. With the rain hitting the roof and the duvet pulled up tight, I fall into an easy, satisfied sleep.

6
STELLA

I wake up to the soft patter of rain. The storm seems to have mostly blown over, and a weak light comes through the window. I stretch languidly, my body feeling refreshed and relaxed in a way it hasn't since I first laid eyes on Jared.

I slip out of bed and pad over to the laptop. I fire it up expectantly and can't help smiling when I see the red dot that means there's a message.

I'm not going to make the meeting this morning.

Disappointment pulls at my stomach. After last night, after I did unspeakable things that make me blush just thinking about them, that's all the message I get?

I'm not sure what I was expecting. Virtual roses, confessions of love? Or at least a few kisses on the end of the message.

I stare at the screen, a feeling of dread building in the pit of my stomach.

No problem. Talk later?

I regret it as soon as I send it. Now I sound desperate. Like the one-night stand who keeps hanging around. But surely this wasn't just a one-night stand?

Not that we actually had sex. Or do you count sexting as sex? Or is it even called sexting when you use the message app on a laptop? I stop myself from googling the term for virtual sex via a messaging app on a computer. Who knows what weird places that would take me?

I've felt my connection with Jared grow, but how well do I really know this guy? I've only met him once. Maybe I'm being paranoid, or maybe I've just been really slutty with someone I hardly know. For all I know he's got a hundred women he's sexting.

I stare at the screen for a few more minutes, but he doesn't reply. Damn, I'm not going to hang around waiting for a man to message me all day. I go take a shower.

By the time I'm dressed and sitting down to work, I'm feeling better. I'm sure my instincts are right about him. We had a connection the first time we met, and over the last few weeks it's gotten stronger. He's just busy this morning. I'm sure he'll message me soon.

After responding to a few customer queries, I move over to my work bench where the latest pattern is.

But I can't concentrate. I keep looking at my laptop

or picking up my phone, but my screens remain annoyingly blank.

I gather the fabric samples up and lay them on my bed, trying to choose the ones I like or that I think my customers will like. Plaid looks like it's making a come-back, but I like bright colors. It's what my customers have come to expect.

My phone rings, and I dive to grab it.

"Hello?" I say breathlessly.

"Did you hear that storm last night? It just about brought down the tree in the front yard."

"Hey, Mom." I can't help feeling disappointed, which isn't fair to Mom. I listen to her go on for a while about the storm and how bad it was. The upshot of the conversation is that I'll be going around there once the rain stops to cut down the loose branches from her tree. Since Dad passed away, I help Mom out a lot.

"I gotta go, Mom. I've got a bunch of work to do."

"You work too hard, sweetie. When are you going to take some time off?"

"Yeah, that's what Jared said."

"Who?"

"No one, Mom." I put my head in my hands because I know where this is going.

"Is that your boyfriend?"

"No, Mom."

"How are you meant to find a husband if you work so hard? I'm not saying you shouldn't work; you know

I'm proud of you, honey, but it can't hurt to take some time off once in a while. Go out dancing or something."

"Yes, Mom." It's a speech I've heard a million times.

"I'm just saying, you're almost thirty..."

"I'm twenty-six."

"Exactly."

"Okay, Mom. I'm gonna go now."

"Okay, honey. Let me know when you can do the tree."

"Bye Mom."

I hang up the phone and sigh. I'm suddenly blinking back tears, and I'm not sure why. Damn Jared for making me feel like this.

I never should have let things go so far last night. I shouldn't have mixed work and pleasure. When he does get in touch, I'll let him know it was a mistake. Go back to just business.

My phone rings again, and I answer it without looking.

"What is it, Mom?"

"It's not your mom, I'm afraid."

My heart stops beating. I'd recognize that deep voice anywhere.

"Jared."

"Stella."

The way he says my name makes me wet between the legs. I squeeze my eyes shut tight. *Stay strong,* I tell myself.

"Look, last night was a mistake. I'm sorry it went so far."

There's silence on the other end of the line, so I keep going before I chicken out. "I never should have let it happen. We're business partners, and we shouldn't have done the sexting."

"It's not sexting when you use a laptop."

"Whatever it's called. It was a mistake."

There's a long pause. "Well, that's a shame."

"Yeah, I'm sorry. I think we should dial it back to strictly business."

He doesn't say anything for a while. "Is that what you really want, Stella?"

What I really want is to have him here with me, to talk to in the flesh and to make love to properly to see if it's as good as my sexting fantasies.

"I don't know," I say honestly.

"Look out the window."

"What?"

"Just look out the window."

I pull back my lace curtain and look out at the gray sky. Light rain is falling, giving the trees a bright green look. There's a man standing on the sidewalk in front of my apartment block with a red umbrella. I peer through the rain at the figure, and my heart starts racing.

"Is that you?" I squint at the figure, and the umbrella tilts back so I can see his face.

"I hope you made that reservation."

My mouth hangs open in disbelief. "I thought you were joking."

"After last night I had to see you."

"You came all this way?"

"I caught a flight this morning. You're taking the day off, and we're going on a date."

I can't say anything. I just stand there with my mouth open.

"So are you going to let me in? Because it's raining out here."

7
JARED

She opens the door and I step inside, shaking the rain off the umbrella. She's not wearing the red dress, but she looks just as good in her sweatpants and loose t-shirt.

"I wasn't expecting you," she says, running a hand through her messy hair. "I would have made an effort."

"You look gorgeous." And I'm not lying. The way those sweatpants hug her ass as I follow her into her apartment makes my dick instantly hard.

She shuts the door behind us, and I can't hold back anymore. I pull her toward me, and she gasps at my touch.

"I had to see you, Stella."

"I can't believe you're here."

I tilt her head up so I can see her eyes. "Is that a good thing?"

Her hungry look tells me everything I need to know. "Yes. Yes, it's more than good."

The over-sized t-shirt she's wearing gapes at the collar, and I lean forward and kiss the exposed skin of her neck. "I had to touch you for real," I say as my lips brush against her soft, soft skin.

A tremor runs through her, and she lets out a soft sigh. My mouth moves up her neck until I'm brushing her plump lips.

Her tongue darts out to meet mine, licking the rain off my lips and sliding into my mouth. I press my mouth to hers, savoring the taste of her and the warmth of her, her heat running down my body and straight to my cock.

I press my body against hers so she can feel the affect she has on me. She wiggles her hips against me, and I let out a groan.

"Oh precious, you are turning me on so much."

"I want to make you feel good," she says, sliding to her knees.

She starts to unbuckle my belt, and the anticipation of what's coming sends a quiver through my dick. "You don't have to do that."

She slides my pants down looking me dead in the eye. "I want to."

Her hands dive into my briefs and she slides them down too, so I'm standing to attention before her. Her eyes go wide when she sees my cock. Then she takes the base of it in her hand and positions the tip to her lips.

Her tongue darts out, and I moan in pleasure as she laps at my dick. Her lips slide down my shaft, and it's like a shock wave ricocheting around my body.

Her hand slides around to take my balls in her hands, gently stroking them as her mouth sucks me into her hot, wet heaven.

I wrap my hands in her hair, pulling her towards me every time she slides down my shaft. My balls are getting heavy with cum, and I'm losing myself in the pure sensation of her touch. But I want more for our first time together.

I gently pull her head back until she's looking up at me.

"Stand up." My voice is husky, and she obeys immediately. "I want all of you."

She wipes a finger across her lower lip and gets to her feet. I pull her toward me and crash my lips into hers. I can taste myself on her, salty and sweet. It's erotic and dirty and makes my dick throb with need.

I lead her to the bed. It's covered with fabric samples, and I sweep them to the floor. We fall onto the bed, entwined in each other. I pull her t-shirt over her head and send it flying across the room.

With one hand I unclasp her bra and her tits spill out, heavy and round with pointy nipples. I take one in my mouth, and she moans as my tongue licks at the hard dome.

I tug at her sweatpants and she wiggles out of them, kicking them to the floor. Her hands run over my body as I pull my t-shirt over my head. Wherever she touches me sets my skin on fire.

Her hands move down to my cock, and she takes it in her hands as I slide my hand over her damp panties.

"Let's take these off." I pull her panties down, and now we're naked, her body spread out in front of me. I pause for a moment drinking in the sight of her, her voluptuous curves, wide hips, and round breasts. She's all woman, and she's all mine.

"You ready for me, precious?"

We're lying side my side and I part her thighs, spreading the delicate folds of her pussy.

"Yes, but I want you to see me."

Suddenly she leans up on her elbows and pushes me down on the bed. She climbs on top, straddling me between her thighs.

My dick skims her dark curly hair as she sits back.

"I want you like this."

"Fine with me."

She rises up on her thighs to align her pussy with my dick. Slowly she eases down so her pussy lips are kissing the tip of my cock.

I let out a moan and she smiles, a devious smile.

"Something tells me you like being in control," I say.

Her eyes sparkle. "I like seeing a powerful man come unhinged."

She sinks down a bit, engulfing the tip of my dick, and I groan, tilting my head back.

I love it that she's confident and takes the lead, but I'm not letting her have all the power. I grab onto her ass and lower her down my dick.

Her smile turns to a groan as I full her up right to the base of my dick. She engulfs me in her tightness and we sit like this, our eyes locked, as I rock her back and forth, giving her pussy time to adjust. When I feel her relax, I lift her up to the end of my dick then thrust hard.

She cries out and tilts her head back, her tits pushing outward. I capture a nipple in my mouth and bounce her up and down on my dick as I suck on her tits.

Every thrust is like an electric shock running through me, and I know I'm not going to last long.

I release her nipple and her ass and let her take control. She slows the pace, moaning with each prolonged thrust. Her hand slips around to cup my balls and they're hard as stone, full of cum waiting to shoot into her.

She picks up the pace, her own peak building. Her head's tilted back in ecstasy as she takes what she needs from me, caught up in her own pleasure, getting faster and faster as her climax builds.

I watch my dick slide in and out of her glistening hole as she rides me hard. It's too much to take and I grab her ass again, having to have her. I pull her down onto me, thrusting into her, my animal instincts taking over as my need to release becomes too strong. All there is in the world is her warm hole and my dick slamming into it.

She cries out my name, and her body shakes. Seeing her face in ecstasy is too much for me and I shoot deep inside her, grabbing her ass and impaling her on my throbbing dick. She rubs against me and her moans pick up again, another orgasm coursing through her. My dick pulses inside her until every last drop is spent.

She collapses on top of me and we roll onto our sides, our legs entwined as are our hearts because there's no doubt in my mind. Now that I have her, I'm never letting her go.

"I thought you were taking me on a date," she says sleepily.

"I am. It's a reverse date. We start with the sex and end with the small talk."

She giggles. Then she rolls over onto her elbow to look at me, suddenly serious. "How long are you in town for?"

"That depends on you."

She raises her eyebrows. "Go on."

"I figure this business and any of the other businesses I'm involved in can be done from anywhere in the country or even the world. So where do you want to live? Because I don't mind as long as it's with you."

She lies back on the bed with a wide grin on her

face. “I think I need another orgasm before I can answer that.”

“I can see to that.” I kiss her shoulder and already my dick’s hard again. I doubt we’ll make it out of the bed today, let alone the house, and that’s all right by me.

EPILOGUE

STELLA

Six years later…

I rub my sweaty palms together under the table and paint a smile onto my face as I stare expectantly up at the podium.

"And the winner in online fashion innovation goes to..."

Jared squeezes my shoulder reassuringly, but I'm holding my breath and don't dare look at him.

"Dressing Her Curves."

"Yes!" I jump out of my seat, waving my arms triumphantly, which is definitely not the elegant thing to do at a fashion awards ceremony, and definitely not when you're six months pregnant carrying twins.

Jared scoops me into a hug. "I knew you could do it."

I make my way to the podium, sashaying past tables, making sure I show off the new maternity range. I'm wearing a version of the red dress with allowances made for my new bump. It's still a gorgeous dress, and despite my even bigger than usual size, I feel sexy as hell in it.

The last six years have been a roller coaster of a ride.

When Jared showed up at my apartment in the rain, neither of us knew he wouldn't leave again for six months. And even then it was only for the two of us to move into a bigger place.

We stayed in my neighborhood so we could help Mom out. She loves having Jared around to help with maintenance around the house. Three years ago, Mom met a man and remarried. So we traveled for a while, but eventually settled back in my hometown.

Turns out I'm a small town girl after all. And it's handy to have Mom around to look after the kids.

We have a boy at home, and now the twins are on the way. Our family is growing as fast as the business.

It's now a franchise business with women all over the country signed up. I'm incredibly proud of what we've built together, the business and our family.

I come back to the table clasping my award. Jared is grinning at me, but there's a look in his eye that I know well.

"You want to head back to the hotel?" he asks.

"As long as we can celebrate properly."

"You know success always makes me horny," he whispers into my neck.

We make our excuses to the other people at the table. I rub my belly and feign tiredness.

We leave together, Jared's hand resting on the small of my back and sending a delicious shiver through me.

I may have won the award tonight, but I feel like I won first prize six years ago.

CURVY GIRLS CAN

Do you love your heroines bold, with big curves, big attitudes and big dreams?

Do you love OTT protective men with possessive attitudes, strong arms and a soft heart? Then the *Curvy Girls Can* series is for you!

Short, sweet and steamy insta-love stories about sassy curvy women and the men who love them.

Keep reading for an excerpt from the next book in the series.

Books 1-6 now available in one volume.

ELLIE

CHAPTER ONE

Ellie

I'm wheezing as I climb the hill that leads to my house. It's more of a slope really, but I'm so out of shape it feels like I've climbed Mt. Everest.

The minimart is only a half mile away, but next time I'm taking the car. This body wasn't made to walk anywhere.

I'm just about at my house when a car cruises past and turns into the Jacobs's driveway across the road. I squint at the figure in the front seat. Tall, cropped hair. My mouth drops open.

The man gets out of the car. He's wearing tight jeans and a fitted t-shirt, and even though he's not in uniform, you'd spot him as a military man a mile away. Brennan Jacobs is back.

Leaves crunch under foot, and I jerk my head around just in time to bump my head against the maple tree on our front lawn.

"Get away from me," I mutter at the tree, hoping Brennan didn't notice. I look across the road and he waves at me, which means he probably did see me walk into a tree.

I give him a feeble wave back, and to my horror he jogs across the road toward me.

"Hey Ellie. How are you?"

I'm red-faced from the hill, okay, the slope, and my t-shirt is stuck to my chest with sweat. If I was going to meet my teenage crush for the first time in ten years, I would have preferred to be wearing something less, um, sweaty that didn't cling to my belly.

But he doesn't seem to notice and gives me a wide smile that seems genuine.

"I'm great. How are you?" I give him a big smile back, because he looks so damn good that I can't help but smile. Then I remember why he's back, and my face falls. "I'm so sorry about your dad."

His smile falters, and he looks down. "Thank you. After years of treatment, it was quite sudden in the end."

"I'm sorry you didn't make it back for the funeral."

He rubs his eyes. "I was on a secret operation, and by the time I was back, the funeral had happened."

A thrill run through me because it sounds so James Bond, but I try to act casual, like I'm not completely turned on by his military prowess. "It was a lovely send off."

He look up at me, and damn, his eyes are the softest blue. "Thanks for going along. That means a lot."

"How's your mom?"

"She's fine, considering. She's had a long time to get used to the idea of life without Dad, but I don't think that makes it any easier."

"No, I don't suppose it does."

"How about you?" he asks, changing the subject. "I heard you were away at college."

My heart races at the fact that he's heard anything about me at all. But his mom is the biggest gossip in the neighborhood, so it's hardly surprising.

"Yeah, I just finished my last semester. I've moved back for a while to decide what the next step is."

"What did you study?"

I take a deep breath, ready for the ridicule that always follows my college major. "Art therapy."

He nods. "That sounds really interesting." I study his face for signs that he's making fun of me, but he seems genuine.

"Helping people heal through art. It works well on children." I say.

"Sounds like a noble thing to do."

No one's ever called me noble before, but I just shrug, playing it cool. "Seemed like a good outlet for my art."

The front door to his house opens, and Mrs. Jacobs wheels herself out of the doorway.

"Brennan!" she calls. "Oh, hi Ellie."

"Hi Mrs. Jacobs."

"Did you get the milk, Brennan?"

Brennan gives me a smile. "I better go and get the shopping inside for Mom."

"Bye," I say, watching his ass as he jogs across the road.

He gets to his driveway and turns back to me. "Nice to see you again, Ellie."

I go quickly into my house and shut the door. My heart's racing, and this time it has nothing to do with the steep slope I just climbed.

I've had a crush on Brennan Jacobs since I was eight years old and he stood up for me at the town fete when Carolyn Summers accused me of stealing cupcakes. Which I didn't do by the way.

I mooned over him until he left for the military six years later. He was eighteen, and I was fourteen. I've seen him a handful of times when he's been back on leave, but in the last few years I've been away at college whenever he's been back.

I'm surprised he even remembers who I am.

I race up the stairs to my old room where I've been staying for the last few months.

It's decorated as I left it before I went to college, pink with posters all over it. Mom hasn't had the heart to redecorate it.

I fall down on my bed and hug the pillow like I used to when I was fourteen. Brennan Jacobs is back, and I still have a massive crush on him.

Books 1-6 now available in one volume.

GET YOUR FREE BOOK

Sign up to the Sadie King mailing list for a FREE book!

You'll be the first to hear about exclusive offers, bonus content and all the news from Sadie King.

To claim your free book visit:
www.authorsadieking.com/free

BOOKS BY SADIE KING

Wild Heart Mountain

Military Heroes

Mountain Heroes

Sunset Coast

Underground Crows MC

Sunset Security

Men of the Sea

The Thief's Lover

The Henchman's Obsession

The Hitman's Redemption

Maple Springs

Men of Maple Mountain

All the Single Dads

Candy's Café

Small Town Sisters

For a full list of titles check out the Sadie King website

www.authorsadieking.com

ABOUT THE AUTHOR

Sadie King is a USA Today Best Selling Author of short instalove romance.

She lives in New Zealand with her ex-military husband and raucous young son.

When she's not writing she loves catching waves with her son, running along the beach, and good wine, preferably drunk with a book in hand.

Keep in touch when you sign up for her newsletter. You'll even snag yourself a free short romance!

www.authorsadieking.com/free

Milton Keynes UK
Ingram Content Group UK Ltd.
UKHW010200230823
427286UK00001B/33